E
SO

Sommers, Trish

A Bird's best friend

DATE			
AG 7 '87	JY 12 '90	FEB 22	DE 22 '03
AG 12 '87	AG 7 '90		JA 09 '03
SE 14 '87	AG 16 '90	MAR 14 '96	FE 01 '04
OC 21 '87	OC 30 '90	MAY 17 '96	90 01 '04
		JUL 09 '96	JY 28 '06
NO 10 '88	MY 7 '92	SEP 23 '96	JE 27 '10
DE 6 '88	MAY 6 '94	NOV 30 '96	AP 18 '13
MR 4 '89	JUL 30 '94	JU 10 '97	
MR 24 '89	SEP 14 '94	AUG 04 '97	JE 23 '14
JY 14 '89	NOV 26 '94	AUG 14 '97	
JY 28 '89	SEP 14 '95	MY 20 '99	JA 30 '16
FE 23 '90	NOV 22 '95	JY 13 '99	JE 22 '18
JE 26 '90	DEC 28 '95	JY 15 '03	

© THE BAKER & TAYLOR CO.

CTW
SESAME STREET®
A GROWING-UP BOOK™

A Bird's Best Friend

By Tish Sommers
Illustrated by Maggie Swanson

*Featuring Jim Henson's
Sesame Street Muppets*

A SESAME STREET / GOLDEN PRESS BOOK
Published by Western Publishing Company, Inc. in conjunction
with Children's Television Workshop

One day, Granny Bird arrived at Big Bird's nest with a surprise for him.

"A puppy!" said Big Bird. "And it isn't even my birthday!"

"I know," Granny said with a smile. "But I think you're old enough to have a puppy of your own. Will you take good care of him? It's a big responsibility."

"Sure!" said Big Bird. "It'll be fun!"

"What are you going to name him?" asked Granny

The puppy barked happily. "That's it!" said Big Bird. "I'll name him Barkley!"

"Bark!" said Barkley to show that he liked his new name.

"Come on, Barkley!" said Big Bird. "Let's go to the park!"

"Wait, Big Bird," said Granny. "Don't forget Barkley's leash and collar. Look. The collar has your name and address on the tag. Always use this leash when you take your puppy out."

"I'll take good care of him, Granny," said Big Bird. "Don't worry!"

Big Bird and Barkley walked past Oscar's trash can.

"Hey, turkey!" Oscar called. "Who's the walking dust mop?"

"This is my very own puppy, Barkley," Big Bird told him.

"A dog, eh?" said Oscar. "That's not as great as having a pet worm like Slimey here, but not bad."

Big Bird met his Sesame Street friends in the park.

"Hello, Big Bird!" said Grover. "Who is your adorable, furry new friend?"

"This is my dog, Barkley." Big Bird introduced him proudly.

"Neato!" said Bert. "I'm partial to pigeons, of course, but dogs are good pets, too."

"Barkley," said Prairie Dawn, "meet my dog, Rustler." Rustler barked hello.

"May we play with Barkley?" asked Telly.

"Sure!" said Big Bird. "But he is just a puppy, so be gentle with him."

Barkley had a wonderful time
playing in the park.

He played tag.

He played hide-and-go-seek.

But his favorite game
was baseball.

Big Bird and Prairie Dawn walked their dogs back to Sesame Street.

"It's time for Barkley to eat," Prairie said.

"I'll give him a nice bowl of birdseed," said Big Bird.

"Oh, no," said Prairie. "Puppies have their own special food. They need to eat a little meal four times a day, and they always need a bowl of fresh water." Prairie Dawn fed Barkley and Rustler, and they ate every bite.

"Barkley looks sleepy," said Prairie Dawn.

"He can sleep in my cozy nest," said Big Bird.

"No, Barkley needs a bed of his own," said Prairie. She put some blankets in a box and made a bed for Barkley next to Big Bird's nest.

Barkley curled up in his new bed.

Prairie and Rustler tiptoed out.

"Sleep tight, Barkley," Big Bird yawned.

He was feeling sleepy, too. He crawled into his nest and was fast asleep in a minute.

But Big Bird didn't sleep for long.

"Yowl!" cried Barkley. He was not used to his new home. Big Bird tried everything to help Barkley go to sleep. He sang songs. He read stories. But Barkley cried all night long.

Sherlock Hemlock knocked on the door the next morning. "I say, is anybody home?" he called.

"Good morning, Sherlock Hemlock," said Big Bird sleepily. "This is my new dog."

"Ah! What's this? Through my detective's magnifying glass, I see a small, furry animal with big ears. It appears to be...a dog!"

"His name is Barkley," said Big Bird.

"Pleased to make your acquaintance, Mr. Barkley," said Sherlock. "Meet my dog, Watson."

"It's time to be up and about and take Barkley for a walk," said Sherlock. "You should walk your puppy three times every day, you know."

"But it's raining today," said Big Bird.

"Elementary, my dear Bird," said Sherlock. "One must face the weather for the sake of one's furry friends."

After breakfast Sherlock, Watson, Barkley, and Big Bird walked down Sesame Street. Barkley splashed through every puddle.

"I must be off," said Sherlock. "There are more mysteries to solve. Good-by."

"Good-by, Sherlock. Good-by, Watson," said Big Bird. "Come on, Barkley, let's go visit Ernie and Bert."

"Hi, Big Bird!" said Ernie.

Barkley raced past him into the apartment and
shook himself on the carpet. Then he ran in and out of
every room. He jumped up on Bert's favorite chair.

"Barkley, stop!" Big Bird yelled.

But it was too late. Black, muddy pawprints were everywhere.

"Barkley! Look what you've done!" Big Bird cried. "I'm sorry about the mess, Ernie."

"That's all right," said Ernie.

"Barkley is just a puppy," said Bert. "He doesn't know any better."

Big Bird helped Ernie and Bert clean up the apartment. Barkley helped, too.

Big Bird took Barkley home. He dried his puppy off
with a big towel, and brushed the tangles out of his fur.
"It's time to take your nap now," he told Barkley.
"I'm going to visit Grover. I won't be gone long."

rkley didn't take a nap. He decided to follow Big
. So he squeezed through the fence and crawled out
o Sesame Street.

He was frightened by the traffic.

He tried to make friends
with Herry Monster's kitten.

He looked for a bone in the garden
next to Hooper's Store.

Then he went back home and found
something even better to chew on.

"Barkley!" Big Bird cried when he saw what Barkley had done. "That was my lucky glove!"

Maria, who was out walking her dog, Perrito, heard Big Bird. "What's wrong?" she asked.

"Barkley chewed up my baseball glove!" Big Bird was close to tears. "And I had to walk him even in the rain, and he tracked mud all over Ernie and Bert's apartment, and he cried all night long, and…"

"Big Bird, Barkley is only a puppy," said Maria. "He needs you to take care of him."

"I know," said Big Bird.

Big Bird picked up his puppy and hugged him. Barkley licked his face.

"Don't worry, Barkley," said Big Bird. "I'll take good care of you, just like Granny Bird said."

Big Bird and Barkley played together every day. Big Bird taught him how to sit and roll over. Maria brought a rubber ball for Barkley to chew on.

One day, Granny Bird came by to visit. Rustler, Perrito, and Watson were eating lunch with Barkley.

"How is Barkley?" Granny Bird asked.

Big Bird patted his pet proudly.

"Just fine," he said. "Barkley is the best present I ever got. He's my best friend."